T0104971

BEST INTERESTS OF THE CHILD

BEST INTERESTS OF THE CHILD

PAUL BOUCHARD

BEST INTERESTS OF THE CHILD

iUniverse books may be ordered through booksellers or by contacting:

iUniverse
1663 Liberty Drive
Bloomington, IN 47403
www.iuniverse.com
844-349-9409

ISBN: 978-1-6632-1362-4 (sc)
ISBN: 978-1-6632-1363-1 (e)

Library of Congress Control Number: 2020923094

Print information available on the last page.

iUniverse rev. date: 12/22/2020

For the child advocates

CHAPTER 1

Jim Andrews was steering his high-mileage Honda Civic sedan out of the Bexar County Juvenile District Court in downtown San Antonio. It was almost five o'clock on a Thursday evening in mid-August 2016. With the temperature hovering over the century mark (San Antonio's sixth consecutive day of such temps), Andrews had his air-conditioning on max and—

A ring on his cell phone. He pressed the speaker button.

"The Law Office of Jim Andrews. This is Jim."

"Yeah, uh, how much do you charge for a court-martial?"

"It depends. I generally charge eight thousand for a special court-martial defense," Andrews said. "Double that for a general court-martial. It all depends on what type of case it is. What are the charges for the case you're talking about?"

"Uh, rape."

He took a sharp left to avoid a road blocked by a construction crew. "I'd have to look at the case file and the specifics about the charges. Are you the accused, sir?"

"Oh yeah."

"Well, I'm heading to my office right now. Could you swing by my office, say, six? I'm located at—"

"I know we're you're at. On Broadway Street, between the Verizon and the Church's Chicken. My barracks buddy, Jose, told me 'bout you. And you do divorces, right? I'm facing that too."

"Yes. My areas of practice are criminal defense and family law."

"How much do you charge for a divorce?"

"That too depends, but usually it's a three thousand minimum flat fee, then three hundred dollars per hour after that. Are there any children involved? Is child support in play?"

"Well, when I get this rape thing cleared up, yeah, I want to support Bethany as best as I can."

"Well, sir, family courts use the standard of *best interests of the child* when it comes to child custody," Andrews said as kept his eyes on the road. "And who's Bethany?"

"My soon-to-be ex-wife's daughter."

Andrews paused. "Sir, who are you accused of raping?"

"Bethany. But I didn't do it, sir."

Andrews, without missing a beat, asked, "How old is Bethany?"

"Sixteen."

"How old was she when the alleged rape occurred?"

"Sir, I'm telling you, man, I didn't rape her."

"I didn't say you did. I said alleged rape."

"Uh, fifteen. The case file says fifteen, sir.

"Let's meet in my office at six, okay? In about an hour."

CHAPTER 2

"Come on in. Door's not locked," Andrews said.

Cory Keller walked inside the small law office and immediately saw Andrews, who was dressed in black suit pants, a white shirt, and a yellow tie, adding paper to a printer paper tray. It was just after six o'clock.

"Hi, I'm Jim Andrews." He extended his hand to the potential new client.

"Army Specialist Cory Keller."

"Nice to meet you, Cory. Please have a seat. Can I offer you anything? Coffee? Bottle of water?"

"Nah, I'm good, sir." He took a seat in the large, comfortable chair next to the work desk. "Say, like my wheels?" Keller pointed through the big office window at the black Ford Mustang he had just parked. "It's a 2012 but with low mileage. That's my gift to me for my tour in the 'Stan. Nice, huh?"

"Yes, it's a beautiful car," Andrews replied as he quickly got a good look at not only the car but the young soldier. *This guy looks like a younger version of Kevin Bacon. Lean and muscular.* Keller was wearing loose-fitting shorts and a tight-fitting tank top. He had a cocky smile on his face, and he spoke fast. *This guy can't be more than twenty-two.*

Andrews walked around the desk and sat in his office chair. "How old are you, Cory?"

"Recently turned twenty-one, sir, and you betcha I'm drinking it up. Tour in the 'Stan with the Climb to Glory Tenth Mountain Division. No booze, no porn, no pussy downrange. Hurt my back and right knee during a fucking IED explosion. Doc says I suffered a TBI, and I've got PTSD. I'm going through the MEB/PEB process."

"I see," Andrews said. "Well, I thank you for your service, Cory. And how's the MEB/PEB process going?"

"Slow as molasses. I just got done with the Medical Evaluation Board two days ago, but now my case will go through the Physical Evaluation Board. It normally takes months, but it can be a year or more. My MEB took like a year. Shit, man, I ain't fit no more for service." He paused. "I'm in the same unit as that traitor, Sergeant Bergdahl. He's getting court-martial too. They should fry his ass and leave my ass alone."

"Well, a court-martial will derail your disability process," Andrews said. "It has priority. If I'm your lead attorney, I'll do the best I can for you."

"So it's sixteen Gs to defend me, huh?"

"Yes, that's what I normally charge. Do you have the case file with you?"

"Uh no. Sorry 'bout that, sir. I left it in the barracks. Actually, at Jose's apartment. My battle buddy Jose said you're the lawyer who got Sergeant Ball off recently for his failed urinalysis on account of his pot smoking."

Andrews thought, *We got damn lucky at that court-martial.*

"I know Sergeant Ball too. You know he self-medicates with weed, right? For his PTSD."

Andrews said nothing.

Keller suddenly stood up. "Uh, sir, mind if I pop one?"

"Pop one?"

"Yeah. Smoke a cigarette outside."

"Sure, you can take a smoke break."

"Thanks. I got hooked on cigarettes downrange. See, many of us were going to this shrink who was assigned to the MASH unit

’cause lots of us had trouble sleeping and combat stress and shit. That doc told us the best way to deal with combat stress was to smoke cigarettes and jerk off.” He smiled and pulled out a pack of Marlboros from his loose shorts. “Now I’m hooked on these cancer sticks.”

CHAPTER 3

Upon returning to the office after his smoke break, Cory made it clear he wanted Andrews as his attorney. Papers were signed, and Andrews was surprised when Keller said, "That won't be a problem," to Andrews saying, "Normally, I request to get paid half up front. Can you pay the eight thousand dollars?"

After talking money, Keller revealed his army lawyer was Captain David O'Rourke, something Andrews was pleased to discover given that he had worked well with the young Trial Defense Services attorney on a money fraud court-martial last year.

That was the good news, that O'Rourke was the TDS attorney. The bad news came in the form of Keller revealing, "My court-martial is in eight days."

"Eight days!" Andrews exclaimed. "No way."

"Way."

"I'll have to request an extension."

"Okay," Keller said, smiling confidently. "I'm in no rush."

"And don't discuss the case with anyone, okay?"

"Yes, sir."

"Now, I assume there's a no contact order between you and your wife and the stepdaughter."

"Oh yeah. Me and Lori haven't been living together for a year now, ever since she accused me of the rape. But just last month, she bitched and complained some more to the chain of command. I'm good with the company commander and battalion commander, but we got ourselves a new brigade commander, Colonel Parker, who decided to court-martial my ass. Captain O'Rourke told me a no contact order is pretty automatic."

"Swear to me you won't discuss the case with anyone except with me and Captain O'Rourke. Not your barrack buddies, not Jose, not anyone. Got it?"

"Yep."

"And don't violate your no contact order. Some soldiers do, and the government turns around and adds that to the charge sheet. We don't want to compound problems, right?"

"Right, sir, but it's already on the charge sheet. I remember that. Two charges—rape of a minor and violation of a no contact order."

Andrews was rubbing his chin, thinking. "You've got my business card, and I've got your contact info. Call or email me anytime. We'll meet in a couple of days to discuss your case in full."

CHAPTER 4

Two hours after meeting his new client, Andrews was sipping a Bud Light at Sam's Burger Joint just as Will Owen Gage, a local guitarist, completed his rendering of Albert King's "Born Under a Bad Sign." Seated to the left of the stage, next to the busy bar, Andrews said, "Another Bud Light please," just as his iPhone started vibrating.

A text from his ex-wife, Jennifer.

He looked down and read the illuminated text: "Hey, can you take care of Tiffany for the weekend? Luis and I are headed to Vegas. I'll drop her off at your office by 5:00 p.m. I can pick her up Sunday night at your place. Thanks for covering on short notice. Let me know ASAP. Thanks. Jen."

He texted back: "Sure. 5:00 p.m. works. I'll be at my office. Jim."

As the bartender handed him the bottled beer, Andrews started thinking about how much things had changed for him in the last couple of years.

It was last June when Jennifer dropped the bombshell. "I'm divorcing you. Oh, and by the way, Luis and I are dating."

Luis was Luis Carrasco, thirty-one, son of San Antonio's car king, Javier Carrasco of "Javier Has a Car for You!" fame. With Daddy Javier at the helm, the Carrasco family had a net worth slightly over $1 billion (they always appeared in *Forbes*'s annual issue of America's richest families), all of which meant the tall and slim Luis was one of San Antonio's most eligible bachelors.

Andrews should have always had his radar screen on, but dammit, how could he when he was working seventy-hour weeks? Jen's divorce bombshell wasn't her first, for three years back, she had pulled the divorce card out and proclaimed, "It's either the army or me. You pick. I'm done being a military spouse."

That was when the young couple lived outside of Fort Meade, Maryland, in one of the Washington, DC, suburbs. That was Andrews's second assignment with the Army JAG Corps (his first had been at Fort Hood, Texas, where, one Saturday evening, while out with friends in Austin, he had met the Texas beauty). Andrews was somehow able to finagle out of that divorce minefield, insisting, "We can move back to Texas. I'll get my next assignment there. We'll be closer to your folks."

And it worked, for a while anyway. Joint Base San Antonio it was for the couple, but after two years, Jen's wishes took over: "No more military spouse for me," she had insisted. "San Antonio is nice, but we'll have to move again next year. Let's stay here. It's me or the army. You pick."

Andrews was lucky in that his obligation with the JAG Corps was coming to an end, making it easier to transition to civilian life at the end of his term. Wanting to keep his marriage together, that's exactly what the Nebraska native did—completed his agreement with the JAG, and through a reciprocity agreement between state bar associations, he was able to become a licensed attorney in Texas. San Antonio was now a permanent home, but with a tight job market, numerous interviews, and two job offers with starting salaries hovering around $60,000, Andrews figured he'd be better off hanging up his own shingle and opening the Law Office of Jim Andrews, specializing in criminal defense and family law matters.

With close to $30,000 in savings, a beautiful wife, and a beautiful daughter, Andrews was looking forward to the future. He was also looking for a great downtown office location where he could apply his trade.

That's where Luis entered the picture, for his billionaire father owned a prime downtown building that was leasing out professional office space. With a perfect location and reasonable rental terms, Andrews signed the lease and opened for business.

He accepted whatever cases came his way, charging low fees, and sometimes representing clients no other attorney wanted. (One of his clients was a sixty-five-year-old blind man who couldn't positively identify the dog that allegedly bit him; he and Andrews lost in court, and the blind client couldn't pay the legal fees.) Divorce work was his bread and butter—both military and civilian divorces—sprinkled with criminal defense cases, including court-martials at nearby Joint Base San Antonio and Lackland Air Force Base.

Then one Saturday morning, about eighteen months ago, when Andrews was in his office working on a motion to suppress evidence in a drunk driver case, in walked a tall, suave man, introducing himself as Luis, a newly minted lawyer (he had passed the Texas bar exam three months prior), who was opening up his own shop adjacent to Andrews's office.

"Oh, and don't worry. I don't practice family law or criminal defense," the sharply dressed attorney had said. "My practice is real estate, both commercial and residential. We have a couple of interesting projects going. You know what they say about this city, heh?"

"No, sir, I don't," Andrews had replied.

"Please, call me Luis. The saying is San Antonio is America's seventh largest city and Mexico's fourth largest. Tremendous population growth out there, Jim. Immigrants keep coming in. It's a booming real estate market."

With their adjacent offices, the two relatively young attorneys struck up a professional relationship and agreement: Jim would refer any real estate matters to Luis, and Luis, in turn, agreed to refer any family law or criminal law matters to his neighbor. Mutual benefits flowed from this referral agreement, as Andrews had tons of clients with landlord-tenant issues, while Luis, financially and socially connected, had many acquaintances with marital difficulties. (Criminal law was a different story, for Luis had no referrals for such cases.)

Six months later, the professional, cordial relationship between Carrasco and Andrews switched to the personal side, for it was when Luis started dating Geneva Vasquez, a former Miss San Antonio, that the social-climbing attorney suggested, "Let's take the ladies out tonight, Jim. We've been working hard all week. Whadaya say? We'll make it a double date."

That's how it started, with the two couples—Jim and Jen, and Luis and Geneva—double-dating on the second Friday of the month, which soon turned into every second and fourth Friday of the month.

Andrews took a sip from his Bud Light.

Man, things have changed, he thought. *My radar screen was on, but I missed it.*

With the frequent double dates, Andrews couldn't help but notice Jen, from time to time, interjecting comments like, "Luis looks so successful … What a nice Mercedes he has … Did you know his father is a billionaire? … Jim, maybe you should do real estate law too …"

Then, out of nowhere, Luis and Geneva broke up (Andrews never found out why), and with the breakup, the double dates vanished, replaced by sympathy and concern from Jen.

"Jim, let's take Luis out tomorrow night. Maybe cheer him up. So what if he doesn't have a date? We'll go out the three of us. … I can set Luis up with Suzie—remember Suzie? Maybe we can all meet in Austin …"

Drinking his beer, Andrews thought, *I should have picked up on things. I noticed Luis was more absent from his office. I didn't connect those dots—Luis knowing my schedule, noticing when I was out of the office (I'm sure he and Jen exchanged personal phone numbers and had their many rendezvous).*

He took another sip of beer and noticed Will Owen Gage tuning his Les Paul guitar.

I didn't see it happening. What could I have done differently? Maybe work less? In the end, it is what it is, human attraction. Like Woody Allen said, "The heart wants what the heart wants." Jen left me for Luis.

Last year's divorce was surprisingly stress-free. *At least Jen deserves a bit of credit there.* Alimony and health care insurance for just one year, and joint custody of the then three-year-old Tiffany, something Andrews insisted on. "Wherever Tiffany is, that's where I'm at. No way are you taking our daughter away from me. And I pay for all costs associated with Tiffany—health insurance, dental, child care, dance lessons, all of it." Andrews was firm, his terms nonnegotiable.

When Jen dropped the divorce-and-new-lover bomb on him, he and a small moving crew cleared out his office in two hours the very next day. And before shutting the door, he scotch-taped an envelope on the door's inside, its contents the office keys. Yeah, he broke his office lease, but next-door-rich-boy-landlord's-son was banging his wife, soon to be ex-wife.

The contents of the office would be in storage for just a month, and after staying in a hotel for three days (he had moved out of their apartment immediately after the marriage-ending news), Andrews signed a lease for a one-bedroom apartment off Broadway Street, behind the relatively new 1800 Broadway Apartments building across from the Pearl District and Sam's Burger Joint. Shortly thereafter, he found the tiny office space also off Broadway, a couple of blocks down, between a Verizon store and a Church's Chicken.

"Another Bud Light, sir?"

Andrews turned from his barstool and saw the young, smiling bartender to his left. He quickly took one last swig from his beer bottle, and just as he handed it to her, Will Owen Gage started playing Stevie Ray Vaughan's "Pride and Joy." "Yes," he told her. "I'll have another Bud Light."

CHAPTER 5

It was a Saturday afternoon with the temperature again hovering around the century mark. Andrews and four-year-old Tiffany were both in their bathing suits, enjoying the pool at the 1800 Broadway Apartment complex, for one of Andrews's army buddies, Lieutenant Colonel Harper, lived in the complex, and with allocated swim passes, guests were allowed. Harper, a JAG attorney and fitness buff, was doing laps in the short pool. Off to Andrews's left was a group of residents grilling steaks on the large, common-area grill, and to his right were residents and their guests enjoying sunbathing while sipping alcoholic drinks.

Stretched out on a beach lounge chair, Andrews was going over his notes—and cocounsel Captain O'Rourke's summary report—of the Keller case when Tiffany asked, "Daddy, can I have an orange popsicle?"

"Yes you may, precious," answered her dad, and he reached down into the cooler under the lounge chair and picked out the requested treat. "But only one popsicle. I don't want you to ruin your dinner. Remember, we're having dinner at Fratellos Deli tonight."

"Yeah!" the smiling Tiffany happily proclaimed. She had her mom's blond hair and her dad's blue eyes. "I want mac 'n' cheese from Fratellos, Daddy."

"Okay, mac 'n' cheese it'll be, but only one of these," and he handed her the popsicle. She unwrapped her cool treat and sat at the edge of the lounge chair next to her father's feet.

Andrews, wearing his prescription sunglasses, picked up his notepad and was about to resume going over his notes when he decided to once more skim through O'Rourke's summary report of their client.

An aspiring novelist, O'Rourke once confided in Andrews, "My heroes are Grisham, Baldacci, and Turow. I'm on my second three-year commitment with the JAG, and I'm hoping some of my submitted manuscripts will get picked up for publication so I can be a full-time writer."

Having taken copious notes about the case, the aspiring novelist wrote numerous short, declarative sentences. His two-and-a-half-page executive summary read in relevant part:

> Cory Keller's upbringing is straight out of J.D. Vance's best seller *Hillbilly Elegy*. Growing up in eastern Kentucky, his mother, Karen Keller, who had him at nineteen and later became a victim of the opioid crisis, divorced his father, Lance Keller when he was three. Then she went through a series of live-in boyfriends. With the collapse of the coal industry, Lance, who has no contact with his family, apparently found a good-paying coal-mining job in Wyoming. … Specialist Keller has a sister, Carla, nineteen, who he's close to, and a half brother, Justin Rogers, twenty-four, who he's friendly with. (Karen had Justin at sixteen.) His maternal grandparents, Mary and Stephen Phillips, helped raise their daughter's kids. … Specialist Keller was an average student in high school. He wrestled and ran track and worked part-time at Wendy's. … The reason he joined the army was not because of poor job

> prospects after high school or that he couldn't pay for college or that he just wanted out of Appalachia (these were factors but not dispositive ones). Instead, according to physiatrist Dr. Rosencrantz (case file, TAB F, page 17), Cory Keller joined the army straight out of high school because he had very bad teeth, the result of drinking high-sugar Mountain Dew. Dr. Rosencrantz is of the opinion our client's constant smiling is an obsession over his newfound teeth in the form of high-quality dentures. … Specialist Keller, an infantryman with the 10th Mountain Division, served fourteen months of a fifteen-month tour in Afghanistan where, toward the end of his tour, his convoy was hit by an IED. He suffered injuries to his right knee and right shoulder, and he has been diagnosed with a TBI and suffering from PTSD. Dr. Rosencrantz has also diagnosed him with narcissism. … The 706 report states Specialist Keller understands right from wrong, and he's able to assist in his own defense. Specialist Keller plays softball for his unit team, and I saw him play. He wears a knee brace, and he plays catcher and throws the ball back to the pitcher in an underhand motion. … Specialist Keller transferred to Army North at Fort Sam Houston, Joint Base San Antonio, first to undergo rehabilitation, but when that failed, then it was the MEB/PEB process at the San Antonio Army Medical Center in San Antonio. … Along with his teeth, Specialist Keller's other pride and joy is his 2012 Ford Mustang …

Andrews reached for his notepad to review his thoughts about the case. He noticed Tiffany was sound asleep, curled up on her left side, next to his feet. He stood up, grabbed the beach towel next to the cooler, and, not wanting his daughter to sunburn, gently placed the towel over her.

"Hey, Jim. You good for another beer?" Lieutenant Colonel Harper asked as he was walking around the southwest portion of the pool.

"Yeah, I'll have another."

Harper quickly toweled himself off, then reached in his cooler and pulled out two Shiner Bocks.

"Hey, I think I'm gonna grill me a steak. What are your plans for dinner, Jim?" He handed Andrews the beer bottle.

"I'm taking Tiffany out to Fratellos. Mac 'n' cheese and gelato. You can't go wrong with those. Maybe next time."

"Sure. Hey, how's that court-martial case looking?"

"Well, I've got lots to think about. Yesterday, I sent the judge and the government my motion for an extension. I hope it's granted 'cause I definitely need more time to prepare."

"Who's the judge?"

"Colonel Matthews."

"Matthews is fair about these things. How much more time do you need?"

"I requested two weeks."

"Very reasonable. My guess is he'll grant it."

Andrews returned to his lounge chair, took a seat, placed his Shiner Bock next to his cooler, and picked up his notepad.

Government's case: estranged wife, soon to be ex-wife, Lori Babson, thirty-one. Says she at first heard two people making "the sex sounds" when she came home early from work. Opened the bedroom door and saw Cory and then fifteen-year-old daughter, Bethany, having sex. Literally caught red-handed with his pants down.

Cory denies it.

Is mother believable?

Bethany?

O'Rourke (page 11 of his long report) states Specialist Cory Keller wants to take the stand. Claims his estranged wife, Lori, is bipolar, "but she's never been diagnosed as such."

Accused on stand—*very rare! Be sure in your interviews that you don't ask the ultimate question*, "Did you do it?" Can't knowingly have witness on stand (if he's lying).

Ultimately, choice to testify is his.

O'Rourke states Bethany is a reluctant witness for Government (page 13 of report).

What is our theme and theory of the case? Mother not credible? She made it up? Why would she fabricate such a story?

Create reasonable doubt for the jury panel.

Do we request psych eval for mother? For purported victim, Bethany?

Fifteen years old; off by a year. Age of consent is sixteen in the military.

Mistake of fact? O'Rourke on page 13 wrote Bethany "looks like a young Sandra Bullock—5'4" slim, raven hair. Could pass for 17–18."

Waive opening statement; see what government puts out.

Good move by Keller—he said nothing to CID. Lawyered up right away to the Criminal Investigative Division folks.

No DNA! Hit this hard! This explains why it took more than a year to take this case to court.

No rape kit. Bethany reluctantly showed up five days later after purported event. She took showers in those five days. Rape kit reveals nothing.

The chain of command was hesitant to bring this case to court. CPT Egan was on the fence. Then it went up, and the new brigade commander brought the charges.

List of government witnesses:

Lori Babson-Keller.

Bethany Babson. Keller claims he wanted to adopt her, that Bethany wanted to change her surname to Keller. But he didn't have the time to adopt her. Cory and Lori have only been married for a year or so. She was thirty; he was roughly a month shy of his twentieth birthday.

Dr. Rachel Cohen, a psychiatrist. She'll testify that, in cases like these, victim is confused, and her academic grades plummet, which happened in the case of Bethany. Will Judge Matthews allow this in court? Motion to file? Get with Captain O'Rourke.

Defense witnesses.

No merit witnesses, just sentencing witnesses if Keller found guilty. Keller is sole merit witness if he testifies.

Mother, Karen Keller. Scared of airplanes, doesn't want to travel. Can be telephonic witness. Says she raised Cory to know right from wrong. He's a good son. Has given me money before.

Carla, sister. Speaks well of her brother, Cory.

In the margins, Andrews wrote: "Keller seems to not have any money problems. Ask O'Rourke his thoughts on this."

Many soldiers can testify Keller is a good soldier:

Sergeant First Class Ramos. Four combat tours. Was with Keller when IED struck. Speaks highly of Keller.

Staff Sergeant Robinson. Current squad leader. Says Keller is a top-notch soldier ready to be a noncommissioned officer but for his physical ailments and TBI.

Sergeant Gore. Three combat tours. Keller's team leader in Afghanistan. Big Keller supporter. Can confirm time line of no contact order.

George Lincoln. Christian evangelical preacher. Knew Keller growing up. "Jesus saved Cory," and "Cory is a God-fearing, God-loving young man." Willing to testify in person. Says, "If the government won't pay my travel, I'll pay my own way. Cory has me and Jesus on his side."

CHAPTER 6

Wednesday at 5:00 p.m., Andrews was in O'Rourke's small office on Fort Sam Houston. The two attorneys were going over the Keller case.

"I want to interview the mother and the daughter," Andrews said, sitting directly across from Captain O'Rourke, who was behind his desk. Dressed in a blue suit and long-sleeve white shirt, Andrews had removed his blue tie and loosened his collar.

"Roger, sir. I've got that slated for this Friday, 6:00 p.m., right in this office."

"Good. And you'll have a female soldier in here with us during the interviews, correct? Good protocol to have a female when interviewing a female victim or purported victim."

"Roger, sir. Sergeant Ambrosio, one of our paralegals, will be here with us. I think there might be a social worker with Bethany as well, but not sure if that social worker is a woman or a man."

"Okay, that'll work," Andrews said. "Thank God Judge Matthews granted our extension. At least we now have a bit more time."

"Understood, sir," O'Rourke said. "I concur."

"Now, I have to ask you, Captain O'Rourke. Did our client tell you anything explosive, like, 'Yeah, I had sex with her.' Anything like that?"

"Nope. Not at all, sir. Maintains his innocence. There were some flirty text messages between Keller and Bethany but nothing incriminating, thank God. CID has those texts. That's why the government is also charging our client with violating his no contact order."

"Right," Andrews said. "The violation of the no contact order is an issue, but it pales in comparison to rape. I'll interview Specialist Keller myself next week in my office, and I'll want you there."

"Sure, absolutely," O'Rourke said. "Oh, and, sir, like I wrote in the report, our client wants to take the stand."

"Yeah, I made a note of that when I read it. His choice of course, but it's terribly risky."

"He insists, sir. He's a narcissist, you know."

"Yeah, I made a note of that too."

O'Rourke stood up and walked to his left, then reached into a small brown refrigerator and got himself a bottle of water.

"Water, sir?"

"Sure, I'll have one," Andrews said, and O'Rourke handed him a bottle.

O'Rourke twisted the cap off his bottle and took a swig. "You know what I thought of last night, sir?"

"Nope."

"The whole underage sex thing. Legal age of consent is sixteen in the army. We're off by one year, as the victim was fifteen. Did you know Hawaii has the legal age of consent also at sixteen, but they have a provision that someone fourteen or older can have sex with someone who is less than five years older than them?"

"No, I didn't know that," Andrews said.

"Right. I'm just saying, sir."

"It's a good point, but we've gone over it forward and backward. Our client was twenty, and Bethany was fifteen. She had a fifteenth birthday party last year, fifteen candles on the cake. Our client was there. Photos were taken. He knew her age. He admits it too."

"Right, sir. Goodbye mistake-of-fact defense. As far as the whole age thing, Lori Babson is thirty-one now, and her daughter is sixteen. She had Bethany when she was fifteen. Lori, out of high school, later got her GED, and now she has a pretty good job at Fedex/Kinkos. Worked her way up; been working there for eight years. The point is when I interviewed her, she had a stretch where she kept saying, 'I don't want Bethany to make the same mistakes I made … I don't want Bethany to make the same mistakes I made.'"

"Yeah, I remember reading that in your report, Captain O'Rourke."

"Sir, you can call me David."

"Sure, okay. And you can call me Jim."

"Great. Well, I just find it sort of ironic, sir. I mean, Jim. The full circle thing about the mother and daughter. Like history repeating itself."

"History often repeats itself, David."

CHAPTER 7

"Ah, sir, no worries, man. I didn't violate my no contact order."

Andrews and O'Rourke were interviewing their client in Andrews's office.

"Like I said, sir, she contacted me, Bethany did, with a text. It's so lame, man. I can't believe I'm charged with something I didn't do."

"Okay, Specialist Keller, now let's go over it again," Andrews said. He was sitting behind his desk while Keller sat across from him, and Captain O'Rourke sat off to his left.

"The thing is, sir, the no contact order went into effect last month, July 15 at 1800 hours. It was a Wednesday, and the company commander, Captain Egan, was really busy. I was told to report to the commander's office to be read the no contact order, but there was a line of soldiers ahead of me with other issues, and I was told Captain Egan was constantly on the phone with the battalion commander about some big funeral ceremony they had to prepare for. So I got read my no contact order, and I was handed a physical copy of the paper, at right around 1820 hours. Well, what do you know? Bethany texted me at 6:08 p.m., which violated the order, an order I didn't know went into effect at 6:00 p.m. The text is a bit flirty, that's all. Hey, it's not my fault if Bethany likes me and I'm like a father to her, a father she never had. Sir, I didn't respond to her 6:08 text, but she texted me again at 6:23 p.m. I've memorized my text to her: 'We can't have contact with each other. No phone calls, emails, texts. I've just been issued a no contact order. Applies to you and your mother. If I need to speak to your mother, I have to go through Sergeant Morales. Sorry.' It's bullshit, sir. Next thing I know, not only is that charge on the court-martial charge sheet, but the company gives me an Article 15 for violating the no contact order. They tell me some double thing—I forget—some double crap doesn't attach, and they can punish me administratively for it—that's the Article 15, now it's also part of my court-martial. Complete bullshit, sir. And—"

"Double jeopardy," Captain O'Rourke suddenly said, cutting off his client. "It's true. Double jeopardy doesn't attach. They can give you an Article 15 and court-martial you for it too."

"Yeah, well, sir, it's crap. Captain Egan reads me the Article 15, and I appeal it to the brigade commander, Colonel Black. Boy, I wish he was still in command; he wouldn't've court-martialed me. No way, man. Anyway, Colonel Black said the no contact order was a 'chicken-shit case,' and instead of the seven days' restriction and seven days' extra duty for punishment, he orders me to write an essay on the importance of discipline. I was lucky enough to have a one-on-one with him, and all he told me was, 'Specialist, given the facts, you should have simply not responded to the text. Take myself, for example. I have three hundred emails in my inbox right now. I'm a fucking colonel. I don't have time to read—let alone respond to—every email. Sometimes, you just have to blow people off, son.'"

Andrews and O'Rourke each had copies of the case file in front of them, and everything their client was telling them was panning out. The late reading and notice. The 6:08 and 6:23 text times, the nature of the texts, the Article 15, and Colonel Black's huge punishment reduction.

"Okay, Specialist Keller, we get it, and—"

"That's what I'm saying, sir. Put me on the stand, and I'll explain it away."

"Well, that's really not necessary, Specialist Keller. We've got Sergeant Gore as a witness who confirms you really found out about the no contact order around 6:20 p.m., twelve minutes after Bethany texted you. Your 6:23 text is harmless. I'm not worried about this charge."

The attorneys spent the next thirty minutes vigorously questioning their client:

"Yes, I was there, and Lori arrived early from work because she wasn't feeling well, but nothing happened."

"Yes, we fought that night, but it's all bullshit."

"Why would she fabricate such a story, Specialist Keller?"

"Like I said, sir, I think she's jealous of Bethany's good looks. Plus, she's a liar. I think she's bipolar."

***

After a quick smoke break outside Andrews's office, Keller, back in his seat, informed his attorneys, "Lori filed for divorce two days ago. I was served by a San Antonio Deputy Sheriff yesterday around 6:00 p.m. The sheriff called my unit, and he was informed I was hanging out at Jose's apartment. Me and my battle buddies were grilling steaks and drinking beers. I was working the grill, shirtless, and the cop handed me the papers."

"Specialist, I highly recommend you have a JAG Legal Assistance attorney look over those papers," Captain O'Rourke said, looking directly at him. "Legal Assistance on the installation is handled by the Air Force; they've got a good team of lawyers there."

"Nah, I want both of you to handle this divorce."

Captain O'Rourke immediately said, "I don't do divorces, Specialist Keller."

Andrews remained silent while Keller looked at him.

"Well, you do divorces, right, sir?"

"Yes, but I usually don't represent a criminal defendant while also handling his divorce. I've done it a few times, but it's not my practice to—"

"Well, do it this time, sir. I'm all for one-stop shopping. Your fee is what, like six thousand dollars? I can cough up half that now and the rest next month."

Andrews rubbed his chin. "Well, bring me the divorce papers tomorrow, and I'll look 'em over, and we'll talk. Right now, our focus is your court-martial, which is in ten days. Now, your Class A uniform is in order? Ribbons and all?"

"Roger, sir," Keller said, his cocky smile ever present. "Bought a new ribbon rack and shiny shoes like you recommended."

"Good. Now the three of us will meet on—"

Captain O'Rourke's text message tone, set on high, suddenly sounded off. Looking at his iPhone screen, he held his left arm up in the air, like a running back shoving away a tackler.

"Gentlemen, this just in. A text from Captain Ryan, the trial counsel prosecutor. Says 'David, check your work email.'"

O'Rourke reached down in his briefcase and picked up his assigned office cell phone. He pressed the email icon and saw that Captain Ryan had sent him and Judge Matthews an email message with an attachment.

"I'm checking here, gentlemen," O'Rourke said. "The email reads: 'Your Honor, Trial Defense Counsel O'Rourke. The government, in the court-martial of the *United States versus Army Specialist Cory Vance Keller*, has an additional witness (see attachment).'"

"Who's the witness?" Andrews asked.

"It says here—Justin Rogers."

CHAPTER 8

"What the fuck, man?" Keller said loudly. Gone was the cocky smile. "This is fucking bullshit."

Andrews asked, "Justin Rogers, he's your half-brother, right?"

"Yeah. We're so-so, not really that close."

"Apparently not," Andrews said.

"Gentlemen, I'm still reading the email here," O'Rourke said. "Let me see … uh … there. 'Mr. Rogers's expected testimony will reveal that the defendant told him, on or about December 16 of 2015, quote, "I'm attracted to her," referring to fifteen-year-old Bethany Babson, and specifically that "I'd do her," meaning that he wanted to have sex with her, a minor.'"

Captain O'Rourke was shaking his head in disbelief, and Andrews said, "I don't think Judge Matthews will allow that testimony in court. We'll file a motion to suppress tonight. It's guy talk—locker room bravado."

"Yeah, sir. Right on. It's all bullshit," Keller said, his cocky smile back on.

CHAPTER 9

It was a Tuesday afternoon, and Keller was alone in his buddy Jose Zuniga's supped-up Chevy Impala. Sitting in the driver's seat, smoking a Marlboro, he had parked the car diagonally from the Fort Sam Houston JAG building.

Because he was being court-martialed (the trial was slated to start Monday, in six days) and also going through the MEB/PEB process (though the latter was on hold because of the upcoming trial), Keller was able to do pretty much what he wanted to do. He had no assigned duties; he simply had to report to the CQ (charge of quarters) desk and sign in the daily log by eight o'clock each weekday morning and sign out by ten at night on weekdays. The hours were nine in the morning and midnight on weekends. He was also allowed to wear civvies (civilian attire) so long as he was meeting with his defense lawyer, which he had an hour ago.

He looked at his watch—2:15 p.m. In fifteen minutes, Andrews and O'Rourke would begin interviewing Justin Rogers about his expected testimony against their client. Keller, with the driver's-side window down, exhaled some smoke while he lowered the music volume, one of Jose's Latin tunes. And though his lawyers were confident Justin's testimony—or at least most of it—wouldn't be allowed at trial (the motion hearing on that matter would be held tomorrow), Keller figured he'd come up with a plan B to cover his bases; he always covered his bases.

He wasn't really close to his half brother. They shared a mother, but at a young age, Justin preferred living in Ohio with his biological dad, William Rogers, a heavy equipment operator. At the age of eighteen, Justin, straight out of high school, left Ohio for the oil boom in North Dakota. Roughly once a year, he'd visit his dad in Ohio and his mother, Cory, and Carla, in Kentucky, for two to three weeks. Then it was back to North Dakota as an oil field roustabout, cleaning up sites and equipment and digging trenches.

It was late last year in December 2015 that the hardworking laborer promised himself, "I'll never spend another winter in North Dakota; too damn cold." Back then, instead of a two-to-three-week vacation in Ohio and Kentucky, he made that a one-week break, then headed to Midland, Texas, the mecca of the Lone Star State's oil boom. He secured employment there for the upcoming fall of 2016, then decided to pay a visit to his half brother, Cory, the proud combat veteran army soldier who drove a beautiful Ford Mustang. And during his brief stay in San Antonio, the two half siblings caught up on old times and discussed the attractiveness of Bethany Babson.

***

Keller lit another cigarette. There was a reason he was in Jose's Impala and not his prized wheels: maybe Justin would see his Ford Mustang and figure his half brother was snooping around, which was exactly what Cory was doing.

As his thoughts went back to his discussion and revelations of last December, Cory periodically looked at Justin's old Ford-150 pickup and kept an even closer eye on the main entrance of the JAG building, which also served as its main exit. Right now, Cory's lawyers were asking Justin all about his expected testimony, and when it was over, Justin would exit the building, go to his pickup truck, and drive off. And that's when Cory would tail him.

CHAPTER 10

While Lieutenant Colonel Harper was swimming laps, Andrews was stretched out on a lawn chair next to the 1800 Broadway Apartments pool. Four-year-old Tiffany, in a yellow bathing suit and lying next to her dad, was asleep. It was a Saturday, late morning, two days before the court-martial of *United States versus Army Specialist Cory Vance Keller*, and Andrews was going over the case file. He had his laptop, Post-its, and two highlighters under his lawn chair, and now, wearing his prescription sunglasses and holding a pencil in his right hand, he was reviewing his notes on a yellow notepad.

Opening Statement? Best to waive it.

This is a case of she said (mother, Lori) and she said (alleged victim, Bethany) versus he said (defendant, Specialist Keller).

Is it worth trying to convince Keller not to testify? Strategy—see how things go first, especially our cross-examinations. Then we get a break (or ask for one) and go over things. Decide then.

Theme and theory? Both women are lying? (This is weak.) Lori is adamant as to what she saw. She's mad and emotional. Bethany is shy, reserved, shaky, and speaks in soft tones.

Keller says Lori is jealous of Bethany. Even if she was (who knows?), why would Lori make up such a rape allegation? By marrying Keller, she and Bethany get free health care. Would she make such an accusation knowing she'll now have to pay health care insurance?

What's the motive?

Either Lori's lying or Keller's lying.

He reached down below his lawn chair, grabbed his water bottle, and took a sip.

Damn too bad we can't argue Mistake of Fact Defense; Keller knew she was fifteen.

Dr. Cohen—credible. Says victims like Bethany become withdrawn, and their grades plummet. Those things happened in our case.

Our job is to poke holes in government's arguments. Create doubt. Emphasize reasonable doubt. It is reasonable to doubt the government's claims when … there's no DNA, a rape kit with no results (Bethany did the exam some five days later after bathing regularly the days prior). … The mother is not a credible witness …

This case is about trust and belief. Who do you believe? Lori/Bethany or combat soldier Specialist Cory Keller?

Andrews flipped to a page that he had entitled "The Law."

Note: These are policy arguments. Do not argue these in court! (Just something to think about, to ponder over.)

Back in Nebraska, grandpa was seventeen and grandma was fifteen when they got married. (It was a different time then, and their parents had to sign to give permission.)

Kids messing around? Keller was twenty last year. Not old enough to consume alcohol.

Legal age of consent in Thailand is fifteen (but we're not in Thailand). Same with Captain O'Rourke's Hawaii example.

Every criminal defense attorney I know has a copy of DSM-5, the Diagnostic and Statistical Manual of Mental Disorders. Earlier versions of DSM had homosexuality as not only a mental disorder but a criminal one as well—you're gay, you're a criminal, and science says so.

Democratically passed laws in the past claimed, as a matter of law, that African Americans are not people but slaves, property, chattel. Discrimination as a matter of law. Famous case of *Loving vs. Virginia* where courts said a White man couldn't marry a Black woman. Think of John, my only sibling, who married Ashley, a Black woman, five years ago. John would be in jail right now, as interracial marriages were against the law in certain states. The judge in *Loving* case said the laws are based on the laws of God, that God created three races—White, Black, and Yellow—and placed these peoples on different continents, which shows God's clear intent that He desired that the races not mix. Thankfully, in 1967, the Supreme Court reversed the discriminatory marriage laws.

I can't raise these policy arguments; society has to draw the line somewhere, and it has, with the age of consent being sixteen in the military.

Andrews took another sip of water, then started reviewing portions of the case file that were tabbed with yellow Post-its. The game plan for the late afternoon was to take Tiffany out for chicken nuggets at McDonald's and then to her favorite ice-cream parlor, Amy's Ice Creams.

He looked at Tiffany, who was still curled up and napping under a towel next to him, then flipped to the first Post-it tab, the expected testimony of the government's first witness, Justin Rogers.

CHAPTER 11

While Andrews was going over his cross-examination of Justin Rogers, the defendant's half brother was curled up inside the trunk of some older, large car, his hands behind his back and tied up, his ankles also tied up, his mouth taped shut, and a black hood fixated over his head. It had all happened so quickly.

On Thursday, after the session with the lawyers, Justin had exited the JAG building, walked to his pickup truck, and driven back to the hotel (a Holiday Inn Express), where he was staying at the government's expense. On his tail—unbeknownst to him—was his narcissist half brother, monitoring his movements.

Cory couldn't absorb the risk of having Justin testify at his court-martial. Andrews and Captain O'Rourke both had explained to their client that Judge Matthews would allow the witness's testimony that "pertains to the defendant having a sexual desire for the underage girl," and Cory couldn't let that happen—wouldn't let that happen.

How to get rid of Justin? The answer was his trusted army buddy, Jose Zuniga.

Jose, like Cory, was himself a soldier going through the MEB/PEB process (his injuries were a TBI and severe hearing loss in his left ear), but the bulky army truck driver was not from Appalachia, nor was he the product of a broken home. His dad had a good-paying job at an oil refinery, and his mom worked as a customer service representative for a large real estate development firm. The problem was Jose ran with the wrong crowd in his native Houston, and his criminal ways stayed with him during his thus far short stint in the army. He ran drugs, McAllen to Houston, McAllen to San Antonio, Laredo to San Antonio, and sometimes San Antonio to Dallas. It was that latter leg—San Antonio to Dallas—where Cory would sometimes tag along and split the driving duties and $5,000 payout with Jose, which explained Cory's healthy finances. The duo never knew which cartel they were working for; all they knew was to report to a Raoul at a certain warehouse in San Antonio, load up the cocaine (and no way was the duo allowed to make the trek with Cory's Mustang—nothing flashy, go with Jose's old Impala), and make the delivery to another warehouse, this one in Dallas, some three hundred miles away.

Cory mentioned his testifying-brother problem to his barracks buddy, and Jose knew what that meant—place a hit on Justin. Price tag—fifteen grand. With his mounting legal bills to Andrews, Cory couldn't afford the hit fee but promised to pay it as soon possible. "You better come up with the money fast, bro," Jose had told him. "Raoul don't fuck around. When he wants his money, he wants his money."

Cramped in the trunk, Justin felt the ride switch from smooth pavement to gravel as he heard the sound of tires meeting tiny pebbles. Earlier that morning, when it was still relatively dark out, he had plans to drive to a nearby IHOP for breakfast. He remembered walking to his pickup when a heavyset Hispanic man, who had parked his car adjacent to Justin's truck, asked if he had any booster cables, "'Cuz my battery died.'" Justin got the booster cables out of his large and locked toolbox and proceeded to bend over under the raised hood of the car. That's when another man (who he never noticed) stunned him with a stun gun to the neck. The two—Jorge and Paco, two of Raoul's associates—placed Justin in the car and sped away, and within fifteen minutes, the unconscious Justin was gagged and bound in the trunk of a different car, heading south.

That car came to a stop, and two other men (Luis and Tony, also Raoul associates) stepped out and opened the trunk. Working as a team, they picked up Justin and started walking to an old abandoned shed. Justin, with a hood over his head, only saw pitch-blackness, but he could feel the hot sun on his body. Suddenly, he felt cooler—because he was now inside the shade of the shed. A certain smell permeated the place, a chlorine-like smell. He felt his legs and the lower half of his body rise, flipped almost upside down, and then he felt his entire body being lifted. His heart began to race, and he started wiggling, but it was no use. The next thing he knew, his hood was removed, and, flipped almost upside down, he was staring at a large barrel filled with some strong-odor liquid. There would be no more Justin; acid would do the job.

CHAPTER 12

Sunday, the day before the court-martial, had the legal duo of Andrews and O'Rourke working all day, going over everything, plotting strategy, and wordsmithing the closing statement. The war room was Andrews's office, lunch was delivery pizza (shared with four-year-old Tiffany, who played with her dolls), while dinner was take-out Chinese food.

Two miles away, Specialist Keller, hanging out at Jose's apartment, was doing his best to relax by drinking beer, shooting pool, and playing video games. About once an hour, in violation of his no contact order, he would text Bethany.

He was always violating his no contact order (the narcissist always has an answer and always finds a way). A piece of paper prohibiting him from contacting Bethany and her mother, his soon to be ex-wife, didn't stop the determined young soldier from saving his ass, from operating in his best self-interests. Actually, there were two pieces of paper that prevented him from contacting his ex-wife and Bethany: a restraining order Lori had argued for and received from a San Antonio court, stating she "feared her husband" and that he was "a sexual predator toward her minor daughter," and the no contact order issued by his company commander, which was standard army practice given the charges he was facing.

In the case of not being able to contact Bethany, Keller simply bought two new cell phones (one for himself, one for Bethany), solely as devices to communicate with each other. He made sure his carrier was different (his regular iPhone carrier was Verizon, while the two new iPhones had T-Mobile as the service provider). And giving Bethany her new "special-purpose iPhone" was too easy; he simply gave Bethany's phone to one of her friends from school, Lisa Clark, who, when visiting Bethany, gave her the device per Keller's instructions.

While taking breaks from shooting billiards and playing video games, Keller sent texts to his love interest:

"You'll do fine tomorrow."

"Remember, I have feelings for you. I care for you."

"When you testify, say nothing happened between us."

"Hey, I picked up something from my civilian lawyer who told me the court uses the standard of best interests of the child in divorces. Cool, eh? You know I have your best interests in mind, even if your mom and I are getting divorced. And you're not a child, but you know what I mean."

Bethany, on the other hand, was all over the place: nervous, confused, torn apart, undecided, but also giggling at Cory's texts, often signing off with "Ha ha" and "LOL."

THE TRIAL

CHAPTER 13

It took the morning and early afternoon, four hours straight, from 9:00 a.m. to 1:00 p.m., to select the panel, what in the civilian court system is called a jury. Nine members in all, consisting of three colonels, two lieutenant colonels, three sergeant majors, one first sergeant, and one sergeant first class, with the gender breakdown being six men and three women. The president of the panel, like a jury foreman, was Colonel Gisella Butler, an ophthalmologist stationed at Fort Sam Houston.

From his army days, Andrews had learned from seasoned defense attorneys that when it came to panel selections, go with "chicks and Catholics, Blacks and babes," the conventional wisdom being that women, Blacks, and Catholics are, in general, more forgiving, more "defense friendly" than, say, evangelical Christians who operate with the belief that "God will bring His wrath upon the evildoers." The panel's racial breakdown, like the gender breakdown, was six and three: six Whites and three Blacks, with Panel President Butler being one of the African Americans.

That morning, the panel started with eleven members. Two were removed, one by the government and the other by Andrews. Without having to state a reason for the removal because he was using his peremtory challenge, Captain Ryan got rid of Sergeant First Class Boyer, who, Andrews figured, was canned because Boyer, like his client, hailed from eastern Kentucky, Appalachia. (Maybe the Hillbillies stick together? The government can't risk that.) As for the defense, Andrews got rid of Lieutenant Colonel Deidra Farrows, a registered nurse, who said, "Yes," when all the panel members were asked, "Have any of you ever been the victim of an inappropriate sexual act?" Later, when she was brought out alone to the panel section and asked to further explain what she had been a victim of, Lieutenant Colonel Farrows responded, "I was raped by my father when I was thirteen." With those words, Colonel Matthews, the presiding judge, removed her from further panel duty, and Andrews, pleased with the panel makeup, had no need to use his peremtory challenge.

CHAPTER 14

Day one of the court-martial ended after the testimony (both direct examination and cross-examination) of Lori Babson. Afterward, Andrews, O'Rourke, and their client met in O'Rourke's office to go over things. O'Rourke was drinking coffee from his mug, while Andrews and Keller each drank from water bottles.

"Well, I think day one went as well as it could have," Andrews said, kicking things off. He was sitting in a chair, as were the others.

"We have as good of a panel as to be expected, and boy did we catch a break when the government couldn't produce their first witness, your half brother, Justin."

Keller said nothing but sported his cocky smile.

"I guess, in the end, he must have had a change of heart and decided not to testify against you," Andrews said.

"Must have," Keller said, still smiling.

"He didn't call you, eh? Or text you? To explain his change of mind?" Andrews asked.

"Nope," answered Keller. "Like I told you, sir, we're really not that close."

"Let's just chalk it up to brotherly love," O'Rourke said. "Specialist Keller, when you next speak to your half brother, tell him thank you. And maybe buy him something he likes. You owe him."

"I will," Keller said, still smiling.

"Well, tomorrow's the big day," Andrews said. "It will all be over by noon, in my estimation. There's Bethany's testimony, then there's your testimony. Are you sure you still want to testify? Both Captain O'Rourke and I are against it. We don't need your testimony to clear you of the violation of the no contact order. We have that exhibit showing the time marks, and we'll have the testimony of Sergeant Gore verifying when you received notice of the order."

"I'm still testifying, sir."

"Well, let's agree to do this," Andrews said. "After Bethany's testimony, I'll ask Judge Matthews for a recess, and the three of us will meet to discuss your testimony."

"Okay."

"And you did well today, Specialist Keller," Andrews said. "Nice uniform, good posture, and no smiling. We can understand why you smiled when the government announced they couldn't produce their first witness, your half brother, Justin. That's a natural response. But remember—no smiling tomorrow, especially if you testify."

"Roger, sir," Keller said, smiling as always.

"Today went well," Andrews reiterated. "We knew your wife's testimony and story. This court-martial really starts tomorrow."

CHAPTER 15

Monday evening. Bethany was in her bedroom, nervous and worried—nervous about tomorrow, about her upcoming testimony, worried about her mom, about Cory (yes, she did have feelings for him), worried about everything. Cory had texted her a few times in the last half hour, but she hadn't responded yet.

Lying on her bed, staring at the ceiling, her mind was racing. Suddenly, she felt the cell phone vibrate.

Another text from Cory.

"Heh, I'm checking up on you some more. You okay? You'll do well tomorrow. Remember, I care for you. I always have your best interests in my mind and in my heart. Luv, C."

CHAPTER 16

"And your professional opinion in this case, Dr. Cohen?"

"Objection, Your Honor," Andrews said. He had also objected to the four previous questions.

"Basis, counsel?"

"Your Honor, the defense once again objects to this government witness's testimony. Her testimony is nonscientific and is based on speculation."

"Overruled," Judge Matthews said. "Please answer the question, Dr. Cohen."

The psychiatrist from the University of Illinois at Urbana-Champaign answered, "That Ms. Bethany Babson exhibits many of the characteristics of a young rape victim."

"Your witness, Defense," said Matthews.

It was Tuesday morning, the second and probable last day of Specialist Keller's court-martial, and Andrews, dressed in a dark blue suit, white shirt, and blue tie, walked up to the podium set up for the defense team.

"Dr. Cohen, isn't it true that you never actually met Bethany? That you never interviewed her?"

"That is correct," she confidently said.

"You never physically examined, Bethany, right?"

"Correct."

"Your entire opinion of Bethany as it relates to this court-martial is based on certain medical and academic records."

"Yes, that's right."

"And those records were composed by other folks, right? Not by you."

"That is true."

"So, you're basing your opinion on your review of other people's work, correct?"

"Well, yes, but—"

"No further questions, Your Honor."

"Government? Rebuttal?" asked Judge Matthews.

"Yes, Your Honor," responded Captain Ryan, who, wearing his dress blue uniform with appropriate name tag and ribbons, approached the prosecutor's podium.

"Dr. Cohen, you are board certified by the American Board of Physician Specialties, correct?"

"Objection," Andrews said.

"Basis?" Judge Mathews asked.

"Asked and answered, Your Honor. Trial counsel earlier established Dr. Cohen's credentials."

"Sustained," the judge said. "Counsel, move on."

"And you have personally reviewed more than one thousand pages about the victim in this case—"

"Objection, Your Honor," Andrews said quickly.

"Basis?"

"Argumentative. It's alleged victim, not victim."

"Sustained. Trial counsel will refer to the minor as alleged victim. Proceed, counsel."

"Isn't is true, Dr. Cohen, that you have personally reviewed more than one thousand pages about the alleged victim in this case?"

"Correct. I have."

***

Captain Ryan's questions to Dr. Cohen lasted for another five minutes, after which he asked Judge Mathews for a fifteen-minute comfort break. With that, Andrews, Captain O'Rourke, and Specialist Keller met in a small office in the courtroom building especially set aside for the defense team. Andrews and Keller were both sitting in adjacent chairs, while Captain O'Rourke, sporting his dress blue uniform like his counterpart, Captain Ryan, was drinking a Starbucks latte.

"Okay, now remember, Specialist Keller, no smiling in the courtroom. You did well this morning. Keep it up. Now Bethany is the last witness for the government."

"Absolutely, sir. No worries," Keller said with a wide, beaming smile. "See, I can turn it on and off, sir." He looked directly at Andrews with a serious but calm look, and then he smiled again.

"Okay, good. I understand you couldn't get the dress blue uniform because Military Clothing and Sales ran out. Maybe we could have gone to Fort Hood, but we were in a time crunch. Plenty of soldiers' best uniform is the Class A. You're looking sharp."

"Thanks, sir."

"Now, after Bethany's testimony, we'll ask Judge Matthews for a recess to go over stuff. We'll assess things at that point. Our case is about creating reasonable doubt through cross-examination. We don't have any witnesses for the merits, except of course if you want to testify. I still urge you not to take the stand, Specialist Keller."

"I understand, sir, but I'm taking the stand."

"What do you think, Captain O'Rourke?" Andrews asked earnestly.

"I concur, sir. Defendant taking the stand is always risky."

"No worries, gentlemen," Keller said, smiling. "We're gonna win this thing."

CHAPTER 17

"All rise," said Staff Sergeant White, the bailiff, as Judge Matthews entered the courtroom. After sitting down behind the raised desk, known as the bench, the army colonel shuffled a few papers, guided his eyeglass frame to the bridge of his nose, and said, "Government, call your next witness."

Rising from his chair, Captain Ryan said, "The government calls Bethany Babson."

Bethany, sporting black dress pants and a white blouse, walked up to the witness stand. Captain Ryan instructed her, "Ms. Babson, please raise your right hand."

She raised her right hand.

"Do you swear or affirm that the testimony you are about to give is the truth, the whole truth, and nothing but the truth, so help you God?"

"Yes."

"Okay. Now I know this is difficult," said Captain Ryan, "but we have to go there, okay?"

Nervous, Bethany nodded and looked down at the floor.

"Ms. Babson, I want to take you back to last year, okay? Specifically, the afternoon of August 11, 2015. Do you remember that day?"

"Yes," she said softly.

Judge Matthews, sitting less than ten feet from her, said, "Ms. Babson, please speak louder and directly into the microphone. The panel members have to hear your testimony."

Bethany cleared her throat and moved slightly forward.

"Ms. Babson, do you know the defendant, Specialist Keller?"

"Yes."

"And how do you know him?"

"He married my mother, but they are now divorcing."

"Okay, and when did your mother marry the defendant?

"Last year."

"When last year? Do you remember the date?"

"Yes. It was May of last year. I think May 12. Something like that."

"And your mother is Lori Babson, correct?"

"Yes."

"Ms. Babson, can you point to Specialist Keller right now for identification?"

She raised her right arm and pointed at Specialist Keller without looking at him.

Captain Ryan said, "Let the record reflect the witness pointed at the defendant."

He then looked down at his notepad. "Now, Ms. Babson, on August 11 of last year, 2015, where did you live?"

"In San Antonio with my mom and Cory."

"Specialist Keller lived with you and your mother last year?"

"Yes. He moved in with us around March, and then they got married a few months after that in May."

"Ms. Babson, now I know what I'm about to ask you is difficult, but we have to go there, okay?"

"Yes."

"Very well. Ms. Babson, on August 11, 2015, did Specialist Keller force you to have sex with him?"

"No," she answered firmly.

Captain Ryan did a double take. "Uh, perhaps you didn't hear me correctly," he said nervously, "so let me repeat the question. On August 11, 2015, here in San Antonio, did Specialist Keller force you to have sex with him?"

"No. No, he didn't," she said.

Captain Ryan paused, unsure of himself. He asked, "Did he have sex with you that day?"

"No."

"Has he ever had sex with you?"

"Yes," she said.

"Okay, I see," Captain Ryan said, now reassured. "Ms. Babson, when did Specialist Keller have sex with you?"

"This year. In June and July. I was sixteen then. I turned sixteen on June 12, and we had sex the next day. I also had sex with him in early July, a few days after his birthday, which is July 5. I've had sex with him twice. I love him."

"Where did this sex take place, Ms. Babson?"

"At an apartment."

"Here in San Antonio?"

"Yes"

Captain Ryan thought about his previous long interview with Bethany. "Ms. Babson, did we—myself and you—meet last week in my office with Captain Hinshaw, the nurse, and discuss this case? Remember that?"

"Yes."

"And isn't it true that last week you told me that last year, when you were fifteen years of age, the defendant raped you here in San Antonio?"

"Yes," she replied shyly.

Captain Ryan asked, "Well, Ms. Babson, which testimony is correct? Last week's statement to me or your testimony now, today's testimony?"

"Today's testimony."

Captain Ryan took a deep breath. "Your Honor, the government respectfully requests a thirty-minute break."

Judge Matthews looked at his watch. "This court-martial is in recess until ten thirty," he said. Then he struck his gavel.

CHAPTER 18

The trio of Keller, Captain O'Rourke, and Andrews were in their assigned separate office for the defense team. O'Rourke and Keller had just high-fived each other.

"That's what I'm talking about," Keller said, smiling.

"We're not off the hook just yet," Andrews said, pacing around the office. "Captain Ryan might be able to rehabilitate Bethany. We don't know, but it's a helluva development, Bethany changing her testimony."

"Yeah," said Captain O'Rourke while nodding in approval, and Keller just kept pacing and smiling.

"I'll base my cross-examination on how things shake out."

"That's a good plan, sir," O'Rourke said.

"Heck, I think I might not even cross-examine her. Leave it all hanging. The gap is there, and it's called reasonable doubt."

"True," O'Rourke said. "Sometimes the best cross-examination is no cross-examination."

"And there's really no need for you to testify," Andrews told Keller. "We'll ask for the break and talk it over, but I can't see why we'd put you on the stand."

"Nah, sir, I'm testifying."

Andrews looked at his client. He shook his head in disappointment and said, "You can't be serious."

"Dead serious, sir. I'll confirm her testimony. Bethany's. Plus, I'll explain away the bullshit about violating the no contact order."

Andrews looked at Keller, then he looked at O'Rourke. "Well, that might work. We'll see."

Keller stopped pacing and asked, "Sir, can I go see my sister and Pastor Lincoln?"

The two defense witnesses had arrived in San Antonio late last night from Kentucky and were to testify during the sentencing phase if Keller was found guilty. Both Carla and Pastor Lincoln were in an office next to the courtroom, an office set aside for defense witnesses.

CHAPTER 19

"Government, call your witness," Judge Matthews said. It was ten thirty sharp.

"The government calls Ms. Lori Babson," said Captain Ryan. During the break, Bethany wouldn't budge on her newfound version of events. It was useless to try to change her mind and her testimony. Captain Ryan could only go back to his key witness.

"Counsel, does this mean your direct examination of Ms. Bethany Babson has terminated and is complete?"

"That's correct, Your Honor."

Judge Matthews frowned and rubbed his chin. He asked, "Defense, do you desire to cross-examine Ms. Bethany Babson?"

Andrews stood up. "Your Honor, the defense reserves the right to cross-examine Ms. Bethany Babson at a later time, if need be."

"Fair enough," Judge Matthews said. "Bailiff, allow the witness, Ms. Lori Babson, to enter the courtroom."

***

Captain Ryan asked Lori a question about time and place, and Andrews immediately said, "Objection, Your Honor."

"Basis?"

"Asked and answered, Your Honor. We've already heard from this witness."

"Government, can you proffer the witness's testimony?"

Flustered, Captain Ryan replied, "Your Honor, we called back this witness to establish what she saw take place last year when her daughter was raped by the defendant."

"Counsel, this court has already heard from Ms. Lori Babson. The defense motion is sustained. Ms. Babson, you're excused from testifying at this stage of this trial. Government, call your next witness."

Even more flustered, Captain Ryan looked at his notepad, then at the second-chair trial counsel, Captain Kim. The two conferred for maybe ten seconds, and then Captain Ryan announced, "Your Honor, the government rests."

"Very well," Judge Matthews said. "Defense, are you ready to proceed with your case?"

Andrews looked at Specialist Keller, who surprisingly sported a serious look. Then he looked at Captain O'Rourke, and the trio huddled and whispered. "Sir, I'm ready," Keller told Andrews. "I'll confirm Bethany's testimony, man. This is cake. And the no contact order, I can explain that too."

"It's your decision, Specialist Keller," Andrews whispered. "I just wanted to ask you questions about the no contact order, but we'll get into the rape charge too. Just remember—serious tone, exude confidence and honesty, and make it businesslike. Just answer my questions, okay?"

"Roger, sir."

Andrews cleared his throat. "Your Honor, the defense calls the defendant, Specialist Cory Keller."

***

Keller was sworn in by Captain Ryan, and he took the witness stand.

The next twenty minutes were filled with Andrews asking Specialist Keller a slew of questions about Charge II of the charge sheet, his violation of the no contact order. Andrews introduced three exhibits into evidence, and he laid out the detailed time line of when Bethany had actually texted Cory minutes before he had knowledge of a no contact order being in effect. And as to Bethany texting him after he knew of the order, Keller explained his text was simply putting her on notice about the order itself.

Andrews ended the exchange about that charge with, "Specialist Keller, were you punished for your text to Bethany?"

"Yes, I was, sir."

"And what was that punishment?"

"Sir, I received an Article 15. My specific punishment was to write an essay to my brigade commander."

"Very well. Thank you," Andrews said. He then went right into Charge I, the rape charge.

"Specialist Keller, did you rape Bethany Babson?"

"No I did not, sir."

"Did you ever have sex with her?"

"Yes I did, sir."

"When did you have sex with her?"

"This year. What Bethany said in this courtroom is the truth."

Captain Ryan stood up and said, "Objection, Your Honor. The witness is—"

"I know where you're going with this, counsel," Judge Matthews said. "The witness cannot inject comments after his testimony. Panel members, ignore defendant's comment about his thoughts of the truthfulness of Ms. Babson's testimony." He then looked at Specialist Keller. "Simply answer the question, Specialist Keller," to which Keller, with a serious look, said, "Yes, sir."

Andrews went right back into his direct examination. "Specialist Keller, how old was Bethany when you had sex with her?"

"Sixteen, sir."

"And how did you know she was sixteen when the two of you had sex?"

"I know because I vividly remember celebrating her sixteenth birthday and my twenty-first birthday. Her mother and I—we're going through a divorce right now—bought her a cake with fifteen candles on it last year when she turned fifteen. This year, two months ago, we celebrated her sixteenth birthday on June 12, and we had sex the next day on June 13. My birthday is July 5. We had sex after my twenty-first birthday, on July 7."

Andrews then asked, "Was your sex with Bethany consensual?"

"Absolutely, sir. I love her, and she loves me."

Andrews left the podium and briefly returned to the defense desk for a quick sip of water. He was done with his direct examination of his client, but he had one more question for Keller—a risky one, one that Captain Ryan would and should object to. It was a question to close all gaps, seal everything up, answer all the possibilities. He quickly glanced at Captain Ryan, who looked tired, weak, and defeated.

"Specialist Keller, I only have one more question for you," he said quickly. "Why would your wife testify that you raped Bethany?"

"Because she's jealous of her daughter's beauty, and she makes things up."

Andrews, surprised there was no objection, said, "No further questions, Your Honor."

"Government, cross-examination of the defendant?" asked Judge Matthews.

Captain Ryan stood up and said, "No cross-examination of this witness, Your Honor."

"Very well. Specialist Keller, you may return to the defense table."

"Thank you, sir," said Specialist Keller.

Andrews would call the final defense witness in the form of Sergeant Gore, the noncommissioned officer who would testify as to the truthfulness of the facts and the time line of Specialist Keller's violation of his no contact order. After fifteen minutes of the corroborating testimony, Andrews ended his direct examination, which was followed by Captain Ryan's brief cross-examination that forced Sergeant Gore to admit, "I am not the decision maker when it comes to Article 15 punishments. That's a commander's job."

With the end of Captain Ryan's cross-examination, Judge Matthews asked, "Rebuttal, Mr. Andrews?" to which Andrews replied, "None, Your Honor."

"Very well," said Matthews. "Defense, do you have another merit witness to call?"

"We do not, Your Honor."

"Does this end your case in chief?"

"It does, Your Honor. The defense rests."

"Very well," Matthews said. He looked at his watch. "I think it's a convenient time for a lunch break. This court-martial is in recess, and we'll reconvene at one thirty for closing arguments."

CHAPTER 20

At three o'clock, Andrews, Keller, and O'Rourke were in their designated office within the courtroom building. Lunch had taken place in the parking lot of the Burger King at Fort Sam Houston inside Andrews's Honda Civic after the trio had gone through the drive-through. The three ate quietly, with Andrews intermittingly taking breaks and going over his closing argument with O'Rourke, while Keller, camped in the back seat, munched on his Whopper and fries and rejoiced in his good fortune. At times, after draining some of his soda, he'd remark, "We got this in the bag, fellas. Freebird coming up."

***

In his closing argument, the young Captain Ryan did his best to emphasize the mother's testimony was the truth, while her daughter's was false. His counterpart, Andrews, argued the opposite, stressing that not one but two witnesses "corroborated the same version of events," and that "the law, as written on the charge sheet, has not been violated." And as to the second charge, Andrews argued, "Panel members, we the defense submit that a no contact order has not been violated when the defendant, after just a few minutes of knowing the very existence of the order and its contents, is contacted by someone via text message and simply texts back, 'I can't have contact with you.' What the facts show is the defendant's newfound knowledge of the order and his intent to comply with its terms. It shows knowledge, intent to comply, and notice to the other person. With that, we submit the second charge, the alleged violation of the no contact order, is government overreach." Andrews paused after saying those words. Then he followed with, "If that's not government overreach, I don't know what is."

Andrews shifted on his feet, and ended with, "Members of the panel, we the defense submit that the government has not come close to proving their case beyond a reasonable doubt. One, there's no DNA, so this case is not about science but rather about the credibility of the witnesses and their testimony. Lori Babson claims a certain sexual encounter occurred, but the very participants of that alleged encounter say this: 'Yeah, it occurred, yes, we had sex, but not when you claim it occurred.' Now, members of the panel, this court-martial is not about science, but it is about logic. Minutes from now, the Honorable Colonel Matthews will read you instructions about the law. Those instructions will include a discourse about reasonable doubt, and when he reads you that instruction, I want you all to think of two things: reasonable inferences and logical deductions. This is not my first rodeo. This is not my first court-martial. Colonel Matthews's instruction will go like this: If I wake up in the morning and I walk outside to bring the garbage bin inside, and while I'm outside, I notice that everywhere I look, I see that everything is wet, then I can make some reasonable inferences and logical deductions. I see my neighbor's roof is wet, every driveway I see is wet, as are all the grass yards—all wet. Here and there, I see small puddles of water, to include in my driveway, and I notice that every parked car is also wet. Now, I didn't catch the weather report last night, and, speaking of last night, I slept soundly. I didn't hear any thunder, nor did I see any lightning, nor did I see or hear it rain. But now I see that everything is wet, and a neighbor's sprinkling system can't explain all the surfaces I see covered in water, to include the roofs of homes. Armed with these facts, I can reasonably infer and logically deduce that it rained last night."

He paused again, then said, "Now let's apply the rules of logic to the case at hand. What's really going on here? Members of the panel, we submit that what's really going on here is a short-lived, failing marriage. And why? Precisely because of what the defendant testified to in this court of law. In a word—jealousy. The mother is jealous of her daughter, pure and simple. Panel members, sexual intercourse did in fact occur, but it was consensual, and that's not against the law."

Andrews paused briefly, then he said, "So strong is our case—we, the defense's case—that we not only request you find the defendant not guilty of the two charges but that, given the testimony of the witnesses, the law and facts of this case, and what transpired in this court of law in the last two days, it is your duty to find Specialist Keller not guilty. Thank you."

***

Now the two defense lawyers waited with their client, waiting for the ultimate verdict. Ten minutes ago, Keller's sister, Carla, and Pastor Lincoln had entered the office to support the young specialist. Lincoln had said a brief prayer, asking for "divine intervention" and that the justice system be aligned with "the way of Jesus the Savior." Carla and Pastor Lincoln left after ten minutes, thinking it would be best to leave Keller—who constantly smiled and looked confident—alone with his lawyers. Sipping from his coffee mug while sitting next to Keller, Captain O'Rourke remarked, "Well, you know what they say: the shorter the panel deliberates, usually it's better for the defense. My watch shows the panel's been deliberating for forty minutes now. Still a short time actually."

"True," Andrews said. "We had a court-martial back at Fort Hood where the panel deliberated for a whole day, something like eighteen hours."

Then, a knock on the door. Captain O'Rourke stood up and walked three paces. He opened the door to find Staff Sergeant White, the bailiff, saying, "It's time, sir."

Keller, Andrews, and O'Rourke walked to the courtroom down the hallway and took their seats behind the defense table. The courtroom was filled with all the witnesses, except Bethany for some reason. Keller, feeling confident, scanned the place and couldn't find her. He saw Lori though—didn't make eye contact with her, but he saw her all right—sitting in the center of the second-row bench, concern written all over her.

"All rise," said Staff Sergeant White when he saw Judge Matthews enter the courtroom.

"Please be seated," said the judge as he took his seat. "Bailiff, please instruct the panel members to enter the courtroom."

Five minutes later, all nine panel members were seated.

"Panel members, have you reached a verdict?" Judge Matthews asked.

Colonel Butler, president of the panel, said, "We have, Your Honor."

"Okay. Thank you. Specialist Keller and defense counsel, please rise," Judge Matthews ordered, and the defense trio stood from their chairs behind the defense table. "What is the panel's verdict, Colonel Butler?"

The tall African American female, dressed in her dress blues and sporting tons of ribbons, rose from her center panel seat. "We, the panel members, in the matter of *United States versus Army Specialist Cory Vance Keller*, find the defendant not guilty of both charges."

"Thank you, Colonel Butler," Matthews said. "Panel members, you are dismissed. This court-martial is adjourned."

Just then, Lori Babson yelled, "Y'all are wrong! He's a rapist. He raped my daughter."

AFTERMATH

CHAPTER 21

After thanking his lawyers and saying goodbye to his sister and Pastor Lincoln (upon her departure, Carla said to Cory, "I guess Justin had a change of heart, heh?" to which Cory replied, smiling, "I guess so"), Keller drove straight to Jose's apartment, where he changed out of his Class A uniform and chilled out like he normally did by drinking beer, smoking cigarettes, playing video games, and shooting pool. Jose, happy for Keller, congratulated him on his acquittal, made sure there was enough beer and burgers for the crew of other buddies that were arriving, and reminded Keller when the two were alone, smoking outside, "Hey, Raoul's been texting me, bro. He needs to be paid for you know what. His texts say he's been texting you too." The comment forced the smiling Keller to check his phone, which included unanswered calls from his mother and two voice mails and six texts from Raoul, the latter two spoken and written in code with the word *beer* replacing the word *money*.

"I'm on it," he told Jose as he texted Raoul with, "I need one week to sort things out. Beer in a week."

As Tony, another soldier going through the MEB/PEB process, came outside to hand Jose and Keller two Bud Lights, Keller received a text: "Unacceptable. Beer due by noon tomorrow. I'm sending two guys to Retaco's for pickup."

"Retaco's," or "Shorty" in Spanish, was the nickname of Paco, one of Raoul's associates. The text meant the money would be paid in Paco's apartment.

Keller, smiling, unconcerned about the text and welcoming the beer, proposed a toast: "Freebird, fellas. Next stop is the MEB/PEB bullshit and return to Fort Living Room civilian life." The three touched beer bottles. Keller then reached into his left back pocket, pulled out his second cell phone, and texted Bethany: "U were great. Though your mom and I are splitting, I will b there 4 u. u r important 2 me. I luv u. Cory."

***

As Keller was chilling, texting, and boozing with his buddies, Captain O'Rourke was back in his apartment with his fiancée, Lynn, enjoying her homemade spaghetti and meatballs, while Andrews, exhausted (he had slept three hours the previous night), was enjoying a draft beer and loaded nachos at Bariba Cantina in downtown San Antonio, where Will Owen Gage was playing with his three-piece band.

Sitting at the bar and still wearing his business suit (he had removed his tie), Andrews was working on his second beer when he felt the vibration of a text from his phone. He reached in his jacket pocket, pulled out his phone, and saw it was a text from his ex, Jennifer.

"Jim, I need to see you tomorrow about something really important. Josephine Street would be a perfect place. How about noon? I'll be there early to ensure we get a table. Let me know. Thanks. Jen."

Josephine Street, a popular old steakhouse adjacent to Josephine's on the edge of the Pearl District (they shared the same owner), was Andrews's favorite restaurant, known for excellent steaks, great drinks, great prices, and great music, even though the latter was not live but recorded.

Looking at his phone screen, Andrews thought, *This can't be good.* He knew his schedule for tomorrow (Smith hearing at 3:00 p.m.; work on Keller's divorce), and with Will Owen Gage playing Albert King's "I'll Play the Blues for You" in the background, he texted back: "Okay. Josephine Street at noon. Jim."

He took a sip of beer and thought about the court-martial acquittal. Great results of course, but there was something troubling. *Calm waters for now, but perhaps rough waters heading our way.*

***

The drive back to the apartment was a dead quiet one for Lori Babson and her daughter. After screaming in the courtroom and being escorted by Bailiff White, Lori gathered herself and spoke with the trial counsel, Captain Ryan, asking him, "How could this happen?" to which the young army prosecutor replied matter-of-factly: "Bethany changed her story. Said he didn't rape her—that they had sex this year, twice in fact, when she was sixteen. Consensual sex."

Exhausted from the last couple of days, her mind racing with various thoughts (*What now? The divorce …*), Lori was driving back home, her daughter occupying the front passenger seat. Too tired to cook, she decided to pull into a Popeye's Chicken drive-through; that would be dinner for tonight. After paying for the chicken and sides, the drive to the apartment took less than ten minutes.

Lori pulled into the apartment complex parking lot and parked in her regular spot. With Bethany carrying the takeout bags, the mother-daughter duo entered the apartment.

"Set the table, Beth," her mother said as the two entered the small kitchen. "I'll get the utensils. Why don't you get the plates?"

"Okay," replied Bethany in a soft, shy voice.

As Lori was removing the comfort food items from the bags, she noticed the dishes that had been washed the day prior, dishes and utensils and pots and pans, spread out and standing upright on the plastic dish rack where they had been left to dry. Bethany picked up two dishes, turned, and started heading to the kitchen table, and while doing so, her mother grabbed a heavy frying pan and—*wham!*—struck her daughter behind the head with it. Bethany, collapsed on the ground, saw stars and felt a powerful, steady, numbing pain take over her entire head. She had dropped the dishes immediately on impact from the blow (one of the dishes broke) and with her right hand felt a bulging bump emerge at the back of her head. She started crying.

"You little bitch," her mother said, standing over her. "Changed your story in the courtroom, huh? I know what I saw, and I know how old you were when I saw it. Probably brought it on to yourself, wearing your short shorts around him, flirting, giggling at his jokes. Pick up some food and eat in your room, bitch. You're grounded too." Lori too began to cry. "I had you when I was barely sixteen," she said, sobbing. Seconds passed, around ten seconds, and then she took a deep breath. "I don't want you to make the same mistakes I made. I thought Cory was different, but I was wrong. You made moves on my man. Now look at the mess we're in."

CHAPTER 22

Keller was outside Jose's apartment, smoking a cigarette. His Bud Light beer was supported by the flat wooden plank on the side of the outdoor grill, and he was cooking himself another burger. Suddenly, he felt his phone vibrate—his second phone, the one reserved for contacting Bethany.

He pressed the text icon and saw a photo of the back of Bethany's head. *Gross ... a visible bump.* Then he read: "Mom hit me with a frying pan. I'm grounded too—not sure the terms of being grounded. It hurts ... I'm scared ... Help."

Keller smiled and thought, *Sweet. Man, my good luck continues. This is fucking awesome.* He texted back: "Call or text your mother's sister, your aunt Lucy, and spend the night with her. I'll handle the rest."

He took a drag from his cigarette, flipped the burger patty, and smiled some more. He pressed the phone call icon and pressed three numbers.

"Nine-one-one, what is your emergency?"

"Yes, I'd like to report a domestic assault."

***

Bethany did as Keller instructed, and in less than fifteen minutes, thirty-three-year-old Aunt Lucy's car was parked in Lori's apartment complex adjacent to a San Antonio police cruiser with blue lights shining. Standing next to the cruiser were Officers Kendrick and Lopez, and in the back seat, red faced with tears rolling down her cheeks, was her sister, Lori.

Lucy, a single mother of two and a Walmart cashier and part-time Uber driver, took responsibility for Bethany until this was sorted out, but for now, the task at hand for the police was to process Lori Babson back at the police station.

***

After the administrative functions at the station, a couple of coffees, the chance to calm herself down, and reassurances from her that she was okay, Kendrick and Lopez drove Lori back to her apartment. The time was twenty past midnight, and with a folder in her hand containing relevant paperwork she had signed, Lori was reminded her court date was in four days.

She entered her apartment, turned the lights on, got herself a glass of water, and sat down in the comfortable recliner in the small living room. She then turned the TV to one of the HBO channels and placed the volume on mute. Her mind was racing.

After a few minutes, she got up, walked to the kitchen, and, opening the cabinet door below the sink, picked up the 9mm handgun. Keller did not know about the gun, nor did Bethany. The gun was always in the same place, was never fired, and served as protection in case there was an apartment break-in.

Her life would end like her mother's had ended, for twenty years ago, when Lori was eleven, her mother, a single mother with two daughters, many intermittent jobs, and even more intermittent boyfriends, took her own life. Lori, handgun in hand, walked back to the recliner and thought things over.

She had lived the life of her mother.

Intermittent boyfriends were also part of her story, but then, last year, she had met Cory, ten years her junior, thinking he was different. The young Kevin Bacon–looking soldier with nice teeth and awesome wheels in the form of a Ford Mustang. And health insurance too! The army was good about taking care of families. With last year's marriage to the combat veteran, her husband would now draw BAH—basic allowance for housing—which covered the apartment rent. Plus, with his regular paycheck, the finances were so much better—money to go out and eat out once in a while, a trip to Six Flags waterpark, stuff like that. But it all unraveled, didn't it? The hopeful father figure turned the teenage Bethany into a love interest. Now the pending divorce, the court-martial acquittal, the frying pan thing, and some court hearing in four days.

She cocked the handgun. It would all be over soon. She pulled the trigger, but ...

CHAPTER 23

Cory slept well that night. Full acquittal, Lori in a mess—things could not have gone better. He dreamt—like he usually did—of his lovemaking with Bethany. The IED explosion in Afghanistan that left him injured—that too would pop up in his dreams, as did sprinkles of his few memories of his growing up years with Justin. Justin was gone—what had to be done had to be done, and his memories of his half brother were just that, memories but with no feelings attached. Same with Lori; he had no feelings for her. But Bethany, that was different. He was in charge, and she would do what he wanted. Always. And he liked that.

CHAPTER 24

Eight o'clock the next morning, Specialist Keller was dressed in his regular army fatigues. With the court-martial acquittal, he figured it was back to light work details, formations to attend, and wait till the MEB/PEB results come in.

"Good morning, Specialist," Sergeant Smith said as Keller signed the daily sign-in log. Smith was the charge of quarters sergeant manning the CQ desk. "Heard you dodged a big bullet. Full acquittal, heh, stud. Always nice to avoid the big cage."

"Yeah. I knew it was bullshit from the start," Keller said, smiling. He placed the pen next to the log.

"Hey, stud, I got some info to relay to you. Company informed me you are to report to Captain Egan and First Sergeant Romero at 0930 sharp this morning."

"Okay. What's this about?"

"Dunno, stud. I'm just the messenger here. Maybe it's about your MEB/PEB and court-martial."

"All right," Keller said, smiling.

With ninety minutes to burn, Keller went outside to the designated smoking area and smoked a couple of cigarettes. He reminded himself that at nine sharp he would call Child Protective Services about last night's assault on Bethany. That too would help his divorce. And at nine thirty, he would meet with his command leadership, whatever that was about.

***

"It's about your court-martial, Specialist Keller."

"What about, sir? I went through the court-martial grinder and came out on top. It's over."

"Well, Specialist," said Captain Egan, the company commander, "last night I got a call from Captain Ryan about the San Antonio District Attorney's Office. A Ms. Sanchez, a lawyer there. She wants to talk to you." He handed a note to Keller with Sanchez's address, suite number, and phone number.

"Talk about what?"

"Beats me," said Egan. "Sometimes their office calls JAG and informs us about coordinating for arrests warrants and serving court papers. But here, Ms. Sanchez wants to talk to you. Now, congrats on the acquittal, but you are to report to her at two o'clock today."

"This is bullshit, sir."

"Listen, Specialist Keller, this is the United States Army. This ain't no Burger King; you can't have it your way. I don't make the rules here. I have a duty to inform you that you are to report to Ms. Sanchez's office at two o'clock today. Now, I also suggest you CYA by CYA: cover your ass by calling your attorney."

***

Outside company headquarters, Keller smoked another cigarette and called Andrews about his two o'clock appointment.

"I thought this might happen, Specialist Keller," Andrews told him. He was drinking a coffee at his office and working on Keller's divorce.

"What is this about, sir?"

"Let me handle it, Specialist Keller."

"But what's it about, sir?"

"Well, let me call the DA's office and find out. I have a hunch, but I don't want to speculate."

***

Keller, like the other soldiers waiting on their MEB/PEB determinations, reported to Building 8 on Fort Sam Houston. It was ten fifteen in the morning, and he was assigned a simple cleanup detail where he mopped some floors and took out the trash. The tasks took him all but twenty minutes. Like the others, the rest of his time was spent watching TV, reading magazines, hanging out, and smoking cigarettes. Usually, these soldiers were given ninety minutes for lunch.

During his work detail, he noticed he was getting constant texts from Jose (reminding him to pay Raoul) and Raoul himself (or maybe one of his associates?) telling him the same. Then, at ten minutes to eleven, Andrews called him. Keller stepped outside to take the call.

"Morning, sir. Gimme some good news."

"I'm afraid I've got bad news, Specialist Keller, but lemme handle it."

"What is it, sir?"

"It's what I figured. Having lost at the court-martial, Captain Ryan immediately called the DA's office. At first, it was the DA's office that was interested in prosecuting your case, based on the facts, but the command leadership, on advice of the JAG office, informed them they would prosecute you with a court-martial. Happens all the time, Specialist Keller. See, the alleged rape happened in your wife's apartment, in San Antonio, not on Fort Sam Houston. But JAG often handles cases like these, so the DA's office, with their heavy load, was more than happy to punt it to JAG for their court-martial prosecution."

"But we won, sir. I was acquitted. Game over, right?"

"Well, Specialist Keller, what I thought would happen did. JAG took the case because the age of consent in the army—the whole military—is sixteen, and the facts, as they knew them, was that Bethany was fifteen when the alleged rape occurred."

"Sir, what is this? It's all bullshit. I went through the grinder and won, man. Freebird."

"Yes, Specialist Keller, but the problem is the age of consent in Texas is seventeen. The way the court-martial played out, we've got Bethany in open court saying she had sex with you at sixteen. That was fine for the court-martial, but it's against state law in Texas. And she testified the sex took place at an apartment in San Antonio, not on the military base. Even if she said it was consensual, an underage participant can't consent."

Keller was shaking his head, his smile evaporated.

"Listen, Specialist Keller. I want you to have some lunch and then see me at my office at one thirty. You will stay at my office, and I'll go to the DA's office alone. Until then, I'm gonna do tons of research on double jeopardy and the mutual jurisdictional agreement between the city of San Antonio and Joint Base San Antonio/Fort Sam Houston."

"Sir, am I gonna be arrested again?"

"I don't know, Specialist Keller. Maybe. They want you to report at the DA's office at two, and maybe that's what they had in mind—to arrest you then and there. That's why I'm going alone. You stay in my office. Let me handle this."

CHAPTER 25

Keller hung up from Andrews's call and lit another cigarette. He noticed in a short amount of time he had received yet more texts from Jose and Raoul. He took a drag, and as he exhaled, his cell phone rang. It was Bethany.

"Hey, what's up, girl?"

"Cory, get me outta here." She was alone, in the parking lot of her aunt Lucy's apartment. "Aunt Lucy is real strict. She has all these rules. And her kids are real brats. I need to get out of here."

Cory thought for a moment as he took another drag from his cigarette.

"How's your head?"

"Better," she said. "Still have the bump, but it's smaller. It only hurts if I touch it. I don't have a headache."

Cory exhaled some smoke. "Pack your stuff, baby doll. I'll be at the parking lot at noon. I'll text you when I arrive."

They hung up, and Cory immediately called Jose.

CHAPTER 26

Noon sharp, and Andrews, dressed in a gray business suit and white shirt, had just parked his Honda Civic in the Josephine Street parking lot. As he entered the popular restaurant, he immediately saw Jennifer at a corner table next to the big tree trunk that was inside the packed eatery, a tree trunk that necessitated a large hole in the floor and one in the ceiling, to allow for the tree to be part of the ambiance. B.B. King's "The Thrill Is Gone" was playing in the background, and Jim ordered an iced tea from the young waitress who was working the adjacent four tables.

"Thanks for meeting with me, Jim," Jennifer said, smiling as her ex-husband took the seat opposite hers. She remained sitting, holding a glass of chardonnay in her left hand. With her blond hair in a french braid and wearing a beige business suit, Jennifer looked great—she always looked great.

Jim, smelling her White Diamonds perfume, said, "Sure. My pleasure. What's up?"

There was an awkward silence, and then Jim, unsure what to say, asked again, "Jen? Jen? Everything okay?"

Her eyes began to tear, and then those tears headed southward on her cheeks, transporting bits of her mascara with them. She placed the wine glass on the table and grabbed a napkin, gently dabbing her eyes with it.

"Oh, Jim," she said in a defeated tone. "I have undisputed information that Luis is cheating on me."

Andrews said nothing, and the waitress arrived with his iced tea. "Are you guys ready to order, or do you need more time?"

"More time please," Jim said. "Thanks."

Still more silence, then Jennifer mustered, "Luis has a girlfriend in Vegas. Of that I am sure. I'm pretty sure—though I'm not certain—that he also has a girlfriend here in San Antonio and one in Austin."

Andrews said nothing.

"I saw photos and many of the texts from the Las Vegas girl." She teared up again.

"I see," Andrews said.

"I'm thinking of hiring a private investigator to confirm what I think is going on here in San Antonio."

Andrews again said, "I see."

"Thank God I didn't have a child with Luis."

There was an awkward silence, and Andrews noticed the song changed to Stevie Ray Vaughan's "Cold Shot."

"Jim, we need to do what's best for Tiffany." She was looking straight at him, still teary-eyed. She blurted out, "I want to leave Luis and have us get back together." She was smiling now, and she held his left hand with her right one. Andrews remained silent.

"It would be best for Tiffany."

He still said nothing.

"I never lost feelings for you, Jim. I … I … it was all a big mistake with Luis."

Again, nothing from Andrews.

"Plenty of couples get back together and remarry."

They would order food shortly thereafter, Andrews settling for a double cheeseburger with french fries while health-conscious Jen went with a chef's salad. While eating, Jen kept pushing her sales pitch of a proposed reunion while Andrews stayed mostly quiet, interjecting an "I see" here and there, absorbing this change of events.

CHAPTER 27

Keller had called Jose to meet him at the apartment. Once there, Jose reminded Keller about the necessity of paying Raoul immediately.

Keller said nothing and changed into civilian attire. He also packed a bag and asked Jose for his car keys and permission to drive his Chevy Impala. Jose, a loyal friend who wanted to please, figured Keller had the payment money and wanted to meet with Raoul's associates in Jose's plain, older car, so he obliged.

"Good luck, bro," he told his battle buddy. "I'll see you later tonight."

***

While Jen and Jim were having lunch at Josephine Street, Keller, recently in possession of Jose's car, was driving the Impala to Aunt Lucy's apartment complex. He knew where it was and how to get there because he, Lori, and Bethany had barbequed there on a few occasions, the last time about three months ago.

As he pulled into the large parking lot, Bethany was there waiting for him, just as planned. (She had told her aunt Lucy she was going out to check the mail, and also, "I'm going across the street to get some lunch at Jimmy John's. Do you want anything? Chips?") Bethany was wearing jeans and a pink T-shirt, and strapped above her right shoulder was a small gym bag and her brown purse. Seeing

Cory pull around, she quickly got in the car, and in minutes they were on Interstate 35 heading south.

"Where are we going, Cory?" she asked as open fields replaced residential buildings. "And whose car is this? You didn't trade in your Mustang, right?"

"Don't worry, baby doll. Got it all planned out. And of course I didn't trade my Mustang. I would never do that."

While driving and sporting his cocky smile, he told her that the destination was Laredo, then "we'll cross into Mexico." With eight thousand dollars in his pocket, the best thing was to "Get the fuck outta the good old US of A." No way was he going back to court on a rape charge. Raoul could wait; he'd make money somehow and wire it to Jose to give to Raoul. And his Ford Mustang, well, he trusted it with Jose. "Maybe we won't stay in Mexico very long. Brazil's the right place for us. We'll stay below the radar screen and ride on buses all the way down to Brazil. We'll look like students."

He had heard about Brazil, and he liked what he had heard. Everything went down there. He would find work there. "We'll be happy in Brazil."

Forty minutes into their southern trek, right before driving under an overpass, Cory and Bethany saw a large digital sign on the side of the overpass: "Child Kidnapping. Black Ford Mustang. Lic. PL #KICK ASS."

Keller smiled and then laughed, and Bethany giggled.

***

Thirty minutes after the kidnapping alert, Keller pulled into a 7-Eleven, one with gas pumps.

"We need some gas, baby doll. Plus, I can use more cigarettes. Need anything?"

"A Coke and barbeque chips," she said, smiling while she was searching for music on YouTube on the iPhone Cory had bought for her; her old iPhone was turned off.

Cory walked into the 7-Eleven, got the items, and waited in line as three patrons were ahead of him. When he reached the cashier counter, he said, "Four packs of Marlboros and twenty bucks on pump six."

Mr. Khan, the proprietor, placed the items (Cokes, chips, cigarettes) in a bag, and Cory handed him a crisp one-hundred-dollar bill.

After getting his change, Cory headed out the door, where a burly Hispanic man asked him, "Sir, would you have any booster cables? My truck is—" All Cory remembered was a sting on his neck and his knees buckling. Roughly ten minutes later, Bethany, with still no sign of Cory, decided to text him. Nothing. Then she dialed his number. Still nothing.

She stepped out of the car, stretched quickly, and walked inside the store. Still no sign of Cory. She then stood outside the locked men's bathroom, where, after five minutes of waiting, out came a tall, bearded man. She went back inside the store and talked to Mr. Khan. He called the police.

CHAPTER 28

Where the hell is he? Andrews thought as he waited in his office. It was one thirty in the afternoon, and there was no sign of Cory. Texts and phone calls to his client went unanswered, and after waiting fifteen minutes, he got in his car and headed to the DA's office to discuss things with Ms. Sanchez.

Just as Andrews pulled onto Broadway Street, his cell phone rang. It was an unfamiliar number.

"Law Office of Jim Andrews," he said.

"Jim. It's Camila Sanchez. Do you know there's a kidnapping alert against your client?"

***

Lori Babson had pulled the trigger last night, but she was unsuccessful in ending her life. With her head all bandaged up after emergency surgery, she was at the San Antonio Military Medical Center, medicated and in and out of sleep.

The angle of the gun to her head had been all wrong, not directly at the temple but angled, pointing forward, the gunshot effectively resulting in a lobotomy. Hearing the gunshot, a neighbor had called 9-1-1. Now here she was, alive, but she would never be the same.

***

While Prosecutor Sanchez was on the phone with Andrews, Lori was semiconscious at SAMMC, Bethany and Mr. Kahn were talking to Officer Morales, and Keller was in the trunk of a car, his wrists and ankles bound, his arms behind his back, his mouth taped shut, and his head covered by a dark hood.

The car stopped, and two muscular Hispanic men got out, opened the trunk, and picked up their victim. They would carry the army soldier about one hundred feet to a small metal shed, where, upon reaching the small, covered building, a chlorine-like smell permeated the surroundings. Cory heard some quick commands in Spanish, and then he felt his legs being lifted up, up, and up, until his feet were pointing directly upward. Upside down, the hood started to come unfastened, and then it was quickly pulled off by one of the handlers. Cory could hear his heart beating, and he was staring at a barrel of some sizzling liquid.

CHAPTER 29

One week later, Andrews was at the San Antonio Family Courthouse in the matter of *The State of Texas in the Interests of Bethany Babson, a Minor.* To his left, on a long, upholstered bench, he saw Bethany sitting in between her mother—the elder Babson was sporting sunglasses on a still-bandaged head and holding a cane in her left hand—and some other lady who he figured was Aunt Lucy. To his right, in the front row, he saw Nancy Vega, the lawyer representing the interests of the state of Texas. He knew Vega from previous child custody hearings.

Andrews's job for this hearing was to simply tell the court that he represented Cory Keller, that his client and Lori Babson were in the process of divorcing, that he hadn't had contact with his client for a week, and that there was a missing person claim filed on his client. He figured the judge, the Honorable Rose Mary Gutierrez, would quote the statutory time limit pertaining to abandonment as it relates to divorces, and once that time period was met—if there was still no sign of Keller—the divorce would be finalized.

Earlier that morning, while at his office and sipping a coffee, he had read Vega's motion, which argued that based on the opinion of two medical experts, Ms. Lori Babson now suffered from severe cognitive limitations that rendered her incapacitated and unfit to be the guardian of Bethany. The motion argued Lucy Hightower was the best candidate for that guardian role.

Sifting through some papers while seated at the far end of the bench, Andrews figured this hearing would last no longer than thirty minutes. As he thought that, Judge Gutierrez entered the courtroom, and Vega and Andrews both stood up.

"Please be seated," she said from her judge's chair. "Good morning, everyone. In the matter of *The State of Texas in the Interests of Bethany Babson, a Minor*, this court will apply the statutory standard of best interests of the child."

***

It was a Friday afternoon, and Andrews decided to take the rest of the day off. He was driving to Fredericksburg, to his favorite German pub for a late lunch, after which he would drive to Austin and hang out at his favorite music venue, Friends, at the far end of Sixth Street, where one of his favorite bands, the Conquistadors, were opening for Jimmy Vaughan and Lou Ann Barton.

As he was driving through the Texas hill country and listening to Will Owen Gage's song "All or Nothing," his thoughts were occupied with his ex's proposition: *Let's get back together.*

Random thoughts kept flooding his mind.

Bad karma, man—what comes around goes around.

The very pain Jennifer is now experiencing is the exact same thing she inflicted on me.

Once a spouse cheats on you, they can't be trusted, and yes, history tends to repeat itself—they'll cheat again.

Would a reunion with Jen work?

Is it worth just giving it a try? Live together for a while, see how things shake out?

And Tiffany. No matter what, I'll always be her father, and I'll always be there for her.

What are the best interests of Tiffany?

What are the best interests of the child?

Printed in the United States
By Bookmasters